This book
belongs to

_____

THE GREAT PIG ESCAPE

Linda Moller

Illustrated by
Donald Teskey

CANONGATE KELPIES

First published 1990 by The O'Brien Press Ltd.
First published in Kelpies 1993

Copyright © Linda Moller
Cover and text illustrations by Donald Teskey

Royalties to Friends of the Earth

British Library Cataloguing-in-Publication Data
A catalogue record for this book is available
on request from the British Library.

ISBN 0 86241 407 5

Printed and bound in Great Britain by
Cox & Wyman Ltd, Reading, Berkshire

CANONGATE PRESS
14 FREDERICK STREET, EDINBURGH

CONTENTS

CHAPTER 1

THE GREAT ESCAPE

THERE WAS NO MOON that night but that was all the better – no-one would see him. The hedgerows were only a shade less black than the sky, and the roadway a shade less black than the hedgerows. It was barely light enough for the pig to see his way, but what he couldn't see he could smell – cabbages in fields, and carrots, cows, cut grass, different hedge smells.

Fifty smells a minute, he was sure of it. Green leafy things … brown moisty things … things to eat … things to roll in.

Suddenly, a beam of light lit up the dark sky, moved across it, then vanished. A moment later it was back again, closer now and brighter. A truck had turned into the road, its headlights full on. There were two men in it.

'Look! What's that on the road?' cried the astonished driver.

'It's a pig! Can you believe it? A pig on the road,' said his companion.

'Well, if he doesn't get out of the way, he'll be a dead pig. He'll be next Sunday's dinner,' laughed the driver.

The pig ran hard, but the truck's lights dazzled and blinded him. In a panic he dodged this way and that.

'Don't run him over or he'll be in too much of a mess to take home. Let's catch him whole.'

The truck ground to a halt and the driver switched off his headlights. The pig could see a little better. He could just make out a high old hedge above a ditch at the side of the road. He bolted for it. The next thing he knew he was falling head-over-heels down a steep bank into the bottom of the ditch. He lay there half-covered with dead leaves and mud under the branches of a tree. The ditch felt safe, but very damp.

Both men leapt out of the cab and ran down the road looking for him.

'Can't see him,' panted the driver.

'Damn! Lost him. He could be anywhere. C'mon, forget him. Let's get back,' said his friend.

The truck drove on again. It passed the pig where he lay in the ditch, too breathless to move.

Meanwhile, an old fox was on his way home. He usually hunted along the hedge because small animals lived under its shelter. He hoped to catch a fieldmouse or a vole or two. As he pushed through the hedge, the smell of pig wafted up to him.

That's strange, he thought, and followed the scent until it led him to the pig.

'What *are* you doing down there?' he barked.

10

The pig looked up, startled. 'I fell in, if you must know.'

He noticed a rather nasty smell, and it seemed to come from the fox.

'Tell me, Fox,' he added, 'what's that smell? Have you trodden in something?'

The fox was quite indignant. 'Certainly not. I'm not so careless. It's not me that smells. I can smell everyone else's smell, so if it were me I'd smell myself, wouldn't I?'

And with that he turned his back on the pig in a huff.

'Sorry, Fox! Perhaps it was something in the ditch,' the pig said to excuse himself, 'but before you go, can you tell me the way to the other pigs? I'm going home!'

'Going home? Why did you ever leave?'

'I didn't want to. Humans took me away. I was a runt, you see — number thirteen — the last of the litter. The sow hadn't got a teat for me to drink from. I was only half the size of the others so I couldn't fight for one. After they'd eaten I'd go round all Sow's teats to get the leftovers. But there was never more than a drop or two.

'Mrs Taggerty, the woman, fed me with a bottle of milk, sometimes. "That runtling," she'd say, "he'll never grow to a decent size. Why don't we just give him away? I hear Stubbs is talking about getting a pig for his boy to look after and to eat up all the food scraps."'

The fox listened attentively, his huff already forgotten.

'Well, in the end I went to Stubbs's farm. Plenty of food there. But I was shut up alone. I couldn't stand it. And his boy didn't like me. All he wanted was a bicycle, a new bicycle. But I found a way to escape. And here I am. Do you think I'm big enough now for the Taggerty's to let me stay?'

'I don't see why not. You're a grand size. But to get to Taggerty's...let me see... that's the next farm to the one after the next. You'll be there before morning. But with those little piggy eyes of yours you'll never see it in the dark. You'd better follow your nose. It's long enough, your nose, you should be able to smell anything half a mile away. Just follow your nose, it'll be easy, easy ...' and the fox was gone.

'Follow your nose. It's easy,' repeated Runtling. But which way should I point my nose to follow it? He never told me that.

But at the thought of finding the other pigs Runtling stopped being tired and scrambled out of the ditch. In front of him the road ran to the right and to the left.

Do I follow my nose to the left or to the right? Which? Thank goodness it doesn't go backwards and forwards too. I know ... I'll close my eyes and turn

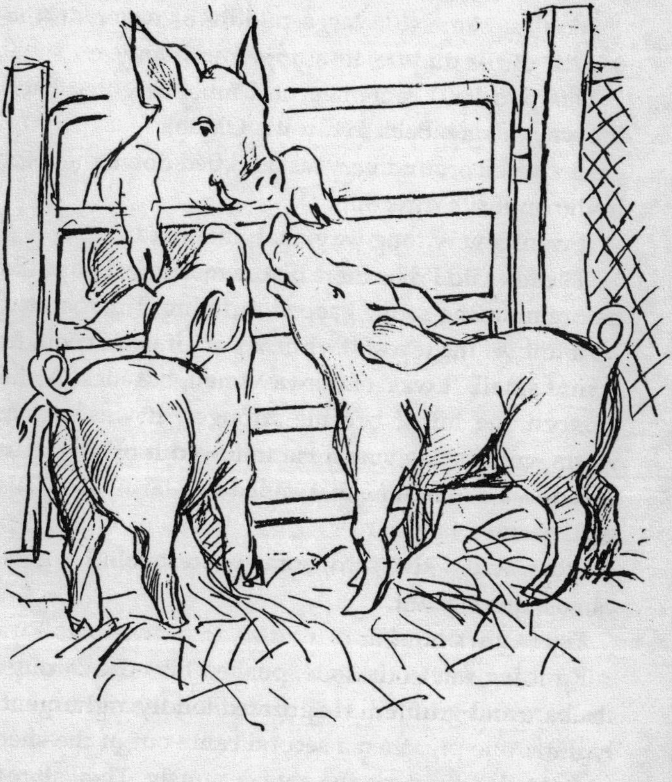

round three times and go whichever way my nose points.

He whirled around three times, then once more just to make sure, and trotted down the road to the left.

Soon he came to a large puddle of water. In the middle of the puddle, he stopped suddenly.

This puddle, I remember it. I must be going back the way I came. Back to my sty. Oh no!

He turned around very fast and fled down the road in the opposite direction.

It went a very long way, that little road.

'The fox said I'd be there before morning, I hope it's before morning soon,' gasped Runtling. The road led up a hill. At the top of the hill, a puff of wind brought a faint smell. It was a far away smell, but nice. As he climbed the hill it became stronger. It was a rich, warm, comforting smell. He followed it off the road and down a long lane that ended in a farmyard. This yard seemed familiar.

From across the yard, somewhere behind a gate, came a quiet grunt.

Pigs! Other pigs!

Runtling ran to the gate, pushed his nose through the bars and grunted. He grunted loudly and urgently. First one pig, then a second came out of the shed and strolled towards the gate curiously. They stared at him. They sniffed him. Runtling squealed with excitement. They rubbed snouts with him. Could they be his brothers? They must be, they must.

But the pigs soon lost interest in him and went back to their warm straw and the comfortable huddle of other sleeping pigs. Runtling pushed against the gate miserably. But it was locked, and for him there was no way in.

CHAPTER 2

THE NIGHT CAT

RUNTLING LAY DOWN pressed close to the gate. It was cold, too cold to sleep. The dark yard was silent ... or was it? Now and again he heard a rustle in the darkness. There were scampering sounds too, and Runtling saw one, then two, lean smooth shapes slide between the bars of the gate.

Rats!

He was sure of it. He knew about rats – always gnawing things. Such long teeth they've got. With those teeth, three of them could gnaw a hole in that gate in no time. A really large hole.

He called to them softly.

'Rats! ... Rats!'

Silence ...

He tried again, very respectfully. 'O Rats! ... O Rats!...'

No answer. But a shape, a large shape and one even darker than the darkness, crept closer and closer to the gate. Runtling's bristles stood up with fear. The shadow edged nearer to him. Now he saw it more clearly. It was a big cat. A black cat. It spoke.

'Seen anything?'

'Oh, you gave me a fright creeping up like that,' shivered Runtling.

'Seen anything?' the cat repeated, her yellow eyes glinting hungrily.

'Yes, I did.'

'What? Where?' asked the cat.

Runtling saw his chance. 'You tell me how I can get into that pigyard and I'll tell you what I saw.'

'Through the gate. That's the only way in. Follow me,' and the cat squirmed easily through the bars of the gate.

'I asked how can I, me, a pig, get into the pigyard, not how can *you* get into the pigyard,' grunted Runtling. 'I'm forty times bigger than you.'

'Forty times! Well forgive me, but that's beyond me, quite beyond me. Sorry,' said the cat, shaking her head.

'How sad,' sighed the pig. He paused, 'All the same, I will tell you what I saw – three rats, three large rats. They went through the gate into the pigyard.'

'Good. So tonight at least, I will eat,' grinned the cat, and vanished into the darkness. She soon reappeared, dropping the remains of a very dead rat.

'Well, one good turn deserves another,' she purred. 'Now I'll tell you something. Keep out of that pigyard. Soon those pigs will be taken away in a cattle truck and they'll never return. They get sold. They're food,

you see. I know. I'm the farm cat. I go everywhere. I listen. I see, and I know.'

Runtling shivered. 'What, my mother too?'

'Your mother? You mean the sow? The one in the separate sty? No, Taggerty keeps her on to breed or there'd be no more pigs to sell ... I say, you're trembling. I suppose I would too if I were a pig your size. But I'm the farm cat. It's the safest job here, you know. But you're not safe. You'd better go, before Taggerty finds you.'

But Runtling didn't go. Where could he go? And he couldn't let the other pigs be taken away in the cattle truck. He must stay to warn them. Then they must plan an escape. The cat had said 'soon'. When was soon? When? The cat would listen and hear, the cat would tell.

CHAPTER 3

HOME! HOME!

EARLY NEXT MORNING Taggerty came across the yard trundling a bin of pigmeal. He was amazed to see a pig lying outside the gate. How did it get out? Had that Jones kid been mucking about in his yard again? He undid the gate.

'Now, get in there,' he shouted. He was about to use his boot but Runtling shot ahead of him and ran in through the gate and across the yard to join the others. Taggerty gazed at him admiringly.

'Hmm! That's some pig. I've done a good job there. He's fattened well.' Runtling was no longer the smallest of the lot, in fact he seemed to be a little bigger than the rest.

Taggerty filled the food trough. As the pigs ate he stood there trying to work out how Runtling had got out. He wondered if a second pig had escaped and wandered off somewhere. Perhaps he ought to count them just to make sure. But this was too difficult right now. The pigs had eaten almost all the food he'd put out, and now they were moving round, pushing and changing places, hoping to find a little more food further down or further up or on the other side of the trough.

Anyway, there seemed to be twelve there, Taggerty decided, and turned to his favourite thought. What price would he get per pig at market this week? Now multiply that by twelve.

But he could never get such sums right when he did them in his head. By the time he'd reached the third or fourth figure, the first two figures had always slipped out of the corner of his mind. They would not be pinned down. It was annoying. He tried three times, then gave up. Never mind, it would be peanuts anyway compared with next year when the new buildings were up. Then he'd be multiplying by fifty not twelve ... add a nought and multiply by five ... but not now.

Those new buildings ... he'd have all the pigs divided into age groups, the older ones below and the others stacked up above them. He could see it all — rows and rows of pigs in easy-clean concrete pens, no straw, no mess, no yard to clean. A proper pig factory.

The van would have to be painted white, with his name on too. 'Taggerty's Tasty Pork, J. Taggerty & Co.' Or maybe 'Taggertys' Tender Pork'? Yes, in green letters with a buttercup or two painted alongside. Though daisies might be better. People liked to imagine that what they ate grew in fields, all naturally.

At least, he decided, these pigs were heavy enough for market now. If he left it any later, they would only put on fat, and people had gone off fat. So this week it was. Market day was Wednesday. And off he went to tell the carrier to call on Wednesday morning.

When the meal was over the pigs came up to Runtling in ones and twos. They couldn't make him out. They pattered around sniffing him but he was looking for his mother.

'Where's Sow?' he asked.

'She's in a sty of her own now, round the corner somewhere. You know, you look just like one of us, and you smell like us. Are you one of us? Are you going to stay?'

'Don't say you've forgotten me! I'm your brother, and I'm home again.' Home, yes. But home was not the same. Sow had gone

The pigs were puzzled. 'Well, why weren't you here yesterday? Where have you been? Tell us.'

So Runtling told them how he had been taken away in a van to Stubbs's farm when he was a piglet. Didn't they notice he had gone?

'We don't remember ... But how did you escape? How did you get out of the pigpen?'

'Well, one night I heard a sharp gnawing and cracking noise at the back of my shed – it went on for hours. The next morning when the boy came to clean out the straw, there in the corner of the wall, was a jagged hole. He bent down to sniff it and looked scared.

'That night the noises started again. Then silence. The straw moved near my trough. And out came an enormous RAT! He was eating the few crumbs I'd left in my trough. I looked at his great yellow teeth and had an idea.

"Rat, it's me, the pig. Rat, would you gnaw a hole in that door for me to escape?"

"Why should I do that?"

"I'd leave you more food in my trough."

"How much more?"

"Lots, lots!"

"Hmm," said the rat thoughtfully. "Agreed! It could be a most useful arrangement. Stubbs has been putting down rat poison in the yard. Some of my family have died of it already."

'The next evening I left him a delicious sausage and some scones from my morning swill.

"That'll do to start," he said and began on the door.

'Just then I heard steps outside. It was the boy bringing my supper. The rat hid under some straw. Nervously the boy opened the door and plonked the bucket of swill down. He must have trodden on the rat's tail because suddenly there was an ear-piercing squeal. The rat jumped halfway across the shed and streaked into his hole.The boy shrieked too and fled across the yard to the farmhouse.

'A gust of cold night air was blowing into the shed.

He'd left the door open! I ran into the yard. Knocked a bucket over. It clattered and clanked and rolled on the cobblestones. The farm dog barked. I ran faster, out of the yard, onto a road, down the road until the farmhouse lights were out of sight...

'But let's save the rest of the story for another day, shall we?'

'But you haven't even told us your name yet,' they said.

'Runtling. That's what people call me. What are your names?'

They looked at each other, hesitating, and started to laugh.

Then one of them said, 'You'll never believe it. I'm Hawthorn – some sort of a tree! And this is Mist and here's Bramble.'

Funny names for pigs, thought Runtling, not pig-like at all.

'Meadow. How about Meadow! That's me!' said another, echoing his thoughts.

'What is a Meadow? What does it taste like?' asked Runtling.

'I wish I knew. I only know there are no buildings in a meadow, just shiny grass, and trees, and the sky above, like that little bit you can see over the gate, there, at the end of the yard. But they never, ever, let us out there. Never. We always have to stay in the pigyard or in our shed. And it's so cramped. We've

24

nothing to do all day except eat. Every day is the same. But you've been outside – all last night – you were running. Tell us about it again, Runtling!'

But two pigs at Runtling's side were nudging him for attention. 'We're Dawn and Dew. But we're usually called the Piglings because we're smaller than the others.'

Then a fine-looking pig faced him. 'Hello, I'm Fern. Runtling, you won't leave us again, will you?' she asked.

There were still five other pigs pushing to get near him. He'd have to try to remember all their names. And he grew more and more uneasy that he had not yet warned them of what would happen to them. Tomorrow? The next day?

Yes, he must warn them that they would be herded with shouts into a cattle truck, driven to the market, then – but the rest was beyond imagining.

Fern was talking to him again. 'It was Sow who insisted on our names and before her Old Sow had insisted, and before her, the Sow of Old Sow. You see the names go back a long time – all the way to the days before pigs were shut up for life in buildings, to the time when they roamed and lived free in woods and commons. The names are things they remembered from the old days in that world. Things pigs must not forget, so that when the time comes to go back to it, they will be ready.

'Sow said that it's still there, that world, somewhere outside, and it's beautiful and that every day there is full of surprises. Today is never quite the same as yesterday. Pigs are happy there. Of course there's food too, food all around them, even under their feet.'

Lovely. How lovely, Runtling thought. And how useless. We're to be killed long before we can ever get back there. Oh, how shall I start to tell them.

He took a long breath.

'Pigs!' he cried. 'Pigs! You and me, we may all be gone tomorrow. Last night while I was lying outside the gate, the farm cat came to me. "Don't try to get in there with those pigs!" she told me. "There's a cattle truck coming to take them to market, to be sold for food. Perhaps tomorrow. Perhaps the day after." So that's all we are, food. That's all we're good for.'

There was a stunned silence. The pigs stared at him, fear in their eyes.

'But,' continued Runtling, 'I couldn't run away just when I'd found you. I had to warn you. We've got to get out of here, and we haven't got long. The cat is on our side. I gave her a bit of help, that's why. And she doesn't like the Taggertys. They don't feed her, but they let her into the house and she hears what they say. She gets to know everything – she said she'd tell me when the cattle truck is coming. So what shall we do? Stay and wait for the truck? Never. Not that. We'll escape!'

26

'But how, Runtling? How?' they cried. 'It's impossible. There's no way out of here and nothing could gnaw a hole in concrete.'

'I don't know how yet. But there's got to be a way. Let's work it out together. But first I think we ought to have a leader. So let's choose a leader – I've escaped myself so I know quite a bit about escapes …'

'Well then, I propose that Runtling be leader,' said Fern. 'All in favour, grunt.' And they all grunted loudly.

Now Runtling knew he was no longer the helpless little pig he had thought himself to be back in his lonely sty. He was quite as big, no, rather bigger than the other pigs. In fact he was quite grown up. Then, too, he'd been in the world outside pigsties. He had had experience. And now he had become a leader. He felt important – even great.

He rose to his full height and faced them all. They waited for his words.

'To the straw. To the straw, to plan the escape,' he whispered. 'We will lie on the straw in the shed as though sleeping a meal off. In the shed we can't be seen or heard.'

'Yes, in the shed one can think better. But there's no need to whisper here, Runtling,' said Hawthorn. 'Because men don't understand our language. They've never understood a single grunt you've said, have they? Never.'

27

The next day the cat slipped through the bars of the pigyard. She had news for Runtling. Suddenly Taggerty lumbered round the corner, and at once the cat behaved as though she were stalking a bird or a mouse. It led her straight to Runtling. There she crouched, staring past him at her imaginary prey.

'Tomorrow,' she whispered. 'The truck. At eleven o'clock.'

Runtling pretended to stare at something a small distance away. Taggerty was now close to the pigyard, but he could hear nothing except the loud squeak of the old wheelbarrow he was pushing.

'At eleven o'clock tomorrow then. All right, be here at suppertime when Taggerty brings the food bin. You'll see something worth watching.'

'I'll be there,' said the cat and pounced. Then as though she had just missed her prey, she rose and stalked away.

CHAPTER 4

THE FALL OF TAGGERTY

ON TUESDAY EVENING Taggerty trundled the pigmeal bin across the yard as usual. And in it was the same pale, boring mixture. He bought it in sacks labelled 'GROWFAST – ALWAYS RELIABLY THE SAME'.

The pigs knew the sound of the pigbin trundling across the farmyard. And they always squealed and grunted loudly at the prospect of food. It was only half-full tonight. Why waste money on big meals when the pigs were to be sold tomorrow, Taggerty reasoned.

Tonight, Taggerty saw the pigs waiting near the gate as usual, but in complete silence. The pigs were not looking at the bin. They were glaring at him – at him! And they weren't moving.

What's up? he wondered. It's so quiet. Why are they all staring at me? What's got into them?

He slowed down, uncertain. It's a bit spooky, he thought.

Then he reminded himself that they were only animals, and what's more, his animals, and he pushed the bin up to the gate. He put it down with a louder

clank than usual, opened the gate and wheeled the bin in. He turned to close the gate.

At that moment Runtling gave a short piercing squeal. That was the signal. Thirteen heavy pigs, bunched together, charged the open gateway. Taggerty stood in front of it. He tried to dodge. Too late. The pigs could no more avoid him than he them. He was knocked off his feet. Down he went, hard, his head hitting the concrete yard.

Through the open gate, across the yard and away up the farm lane, at top speed, streamed the pigs. At the road they turned right, though where that led they had no idea. Runtling was in the lead. They ran in single file keeping close to the hedgerows and the wayside trees, hidden, or so they hoped.

But their presence was already known to some. A late blackbird chink-chinked an alarm call. Far down the road a rabbit raised its head and sat up, nose twitching, then bolted across the road for cover. Three young horses in the roadside field grew curious. They ambled down to the hedge. They thought there was some sort of party going on and cantered excitedly along beside the pigs on the other side of the hedge.

'Go away!' hissed Runtling. 'Go away.'

But the young horses went on cantering around, in their silly way, until the pigs were out of sight.

Close behind Runtling ran Hawthorn. Though Hawthorn could easily have outrun them all, that

31

wasn't allowed – Runtling was the leader. Then came the rest of the pigs. Right at the end behind Bramble came the Piglings. Only fear kept them from lagging behind.

'They turn you into sausages if they catch you,' panted one. 'The cat said so.'

'No, not sausages! It was pies she said. I remember, it was pies. Which is worse, do you think? Sausages or pies?' They were close to tears.

Their fear grew as the road narrowed and walls replaced the shelter of the hedgerows. The grass verge had disappeared too. On the soft grass they had run silently but for a muffled thudding of hooves. Now they were running, thirteen of them, on the hard road.

'We're making an awful noise. Someone will hear us,' gasped one of the Piglings.

'I know, it's our hooves. They clatter …' puffed the other.

Runtling was aware of it too. 'People might hear us before they see us, so even if we try to hide … but there's nowhere on this road to hide, nowhere. What shall we do? Think … think fast.'

But he found it difficult to think fast and run fast at the same time. Besides, he couldn't stop thinking of Taggerty. Was he dead? Or was he even now getting up from where he had fallen with such an awful thud? Maybe he was already through the gate and running after them?

Busy with his fears, Runtling nearly missed seeing that a lane, partly hidden by a clump of trees, led off the road.

'A lane! A lane!' he shouted over his shoulder and turned down it.

It was an old lane with a bank on one side that sheltered the pigs from sight. As they trotted along, the bottom of the lane grew wetter and stonier. Here and there brambles arched over it. They stumbled on. The lane seemed to get narrower and the bank higher. Bracken grew tall and curved into a green tunnel for them. Here they felt safe, and dared to stop and rest for a moment.

A trickle of water usually meandered down the lane. But lately heavy rainfall had turned the trickle into a stream that had eaten its way into the bank, turning it into thick squelching mud. The Piglings, too tired to stand, lay sprawled in the mud.

It was cool and satisfying. They began to roll in it for pleasure. When they rose, their smooth pink backs and legs were a splodgy black.

'Let's all do that!' cried Hawthorn, 'and be splodgy dark. Then we won't show up so much, we'll be ... what's the word? Camouflaged!'

So they all rolled and tumbled in the mud. It was pure delight. Everything else was forgotten until a good deal later when Runtling remembered that he was leader of a great escape. He stood up, black and glistening.

'We must keep going. At night we can't be seen. Night is our one chance of getting too far away for Taggerty ever to find us. We must trot on and on and on through the night. When daytime comes we'll lie up somewhere hidden, and sleep!'

'What about eating?' asked one.

'I'm afraid there's nothing to eat,' answered Runtling.

Silence fell. It was a full day since their last meal and their supper lay spilt all over Taggerty's yard.

The Piglings looked at each other, alarmed. 'Nothing to eat. Nothing to eat…'

CHAPTER 5

AN EVIL SPIRIT

BACK AT THE FARM Mrs Taggerty was sitting on the sofa with her feet up reading the *Oldcastle Weekly News*. She was waiting for Taggerty to come back for supper.

He's very late tonight, she thought. Probably pottering about in the yard as usual! Tinkering with the tractor, I suppose. The tractor had broken down again.

But Taggerty still lay where he had fallen. His head hurt when he moved. He tried once more to get up. He rolled over, clutched the pig-netting fence and managed to haul himself onto his feet. But this made him dizzy and he decided to try crawling instead. He crawled through the pigyard gateway and was half-way across the farmyard when he collapsed, feeling sick.

Mrs Taggerty put down the paper and opened the back door.

'Enough is enough,' she muttered to herself.

She shouted loudly, several times. No reply. Supper was almost cold, so out she swept to look for him.

He was not in the barn. He was not in the tool shed. In the yard she shouted again. Back came a faint, croaky cry, 'Help! Help!'

All he could say when she found him was, 'My head … oh! my head!'

Later, covered with a blanket, and lying on the sofa with closed eyes, he spoke again. 'Did you see the pigs?'

'No, I didn't look at them, why?'

'They've gone. I don't know where. They charged me. They knocked me down. They did it on purpose. You should have seen them all. Standing stock-still they were, with staring eyes, waiting for the moment. Suddenly they all charged, all at once. I didn't stand a chance.'

What a ridiculous story, thought Mrs Taggerty. The fall has knocked him silly. And she rushed off to make him another cup of hot sweet tea.

'Those aren't ordinary pigs anymore,' he moaned. 'Something's got into them. An evil spirit, or there's black magic at work. Don't bring them back here when they're found. I'm not having them back here. Sell them. Sell them off the road. Sell them at any price!'

He groaned and closed his eyes again.

Mrs Taggerty looked into the pigyard herself. Not a pig to be seen, except for the sow in her own sty. So Taggerty's story must be true. She telephoned the police.

'Well, I'm sorry to hear about it,' said the policeman. 'Very worrying for you, I'm sure. But there's only one of us here evenings, and looking for stray animals is not on my duty list. I'll report it to the sergeant in the morning though. He may think that twelve stray pigs are a danger to road traffic and that he ought to do something about it.'

The doctor was called in. He said Taggerty had concussion and must lie in bed very quietly and not think. He'd call again in three days' time.

'But I'm very worried about those pigs. They must be found,' said Mrs Taggerty.

'Not to worry, Mrs Taggerty, not to worry. Twelve pigs can't just disappear,' said the doctor. 'Your husband is more important than his pigs. Now, you stay home and look after him. And if that headache is not better tomorrow, telephone me.'

But Mrs Taggerty did worry: What's best to do? What'll I do? ... Get it in the papers straight away. That's what.

So she telephoned the *Oldcastle Weekly News* and told them the whole story.

'Really?' said the *Oldcastle Weekly News* reporter, 'this is an amazing story. You say your husband was knocked off his feet by the pigs, and it wasn't an accident. They actually attacked him?'

'Yes. Yes.' Mrs Taggerty was most emphatic. 'They did. And there's only one explanation for it. There could only be one. An evil spirit. It entered the pigs. It was giving them orders.'

'Ah, like the Gadarene swine – in the Bible?'

'That's it. Like the Gadarene swine,' replied Mrs Taggerty excitedly. 'Now if that sort of thing can happen once, it could happen again, couldn't it?'

'Well ... I suppose it could,' said the reporter, not believing for a moment that it could. In fact, he found the whole story unlikely ... absurd, and was certain most of his readers would too. But what should he say to her?

'Mrs Taggerty ... er ... I'm afraid it's just too late now to get a notice about the pigs into this week's paper. I suggest you put a little advertisement in next week. You could say "Lost or stolen, twelve pigs. Finder rewarded." Give your telephone number. Now, if you'll excuse me, I must ring off. There's another call waiting for me. Don't worry. I feel sure you'll get your pigs back.'

CHAPTER 6

THE NEWS SPREADS

THE PIGS DID NOT KNOW how far they had come, or whether being hungry was worse than being afraid, or whether being afraid was worse than being hungry.

'There's nothing to eat,' Runtling had said. Yet the night air was alive with smells, some of them mouth-watering. They longed to track down these smells and gobble up whatever it was they came from. But there was no time. They trotted, and ran, and trotted the night through. And now the stars were fading and the darkness had become a greyness.

'We've got to find a hide-out before daylight. A nice wild patch, not farmland. Keep looking, everyone,' ordered Runtling.

'Keep looking,' each pig said to the other.

But they saw nothing. The countryside was too neat and tidy here, small hedges, big fields, pleasant lanes. It was worrying.

Then the Piglings sent word up through the line. 'Would a building do? We've just passed a barn. It's half fallen down, so it must be empty.'

Runtling paused. Yes, a building might do, mightn't it? The barn was behind a few trees only a little way back. They found the door hanging off its hinges, and half the roof had collapsed. There was just enough room in the other half and it had a roof of sorts. The floor was hard, damp and cold.

'There's no straw to lie on,' they complained.

'Well, we'll have to lie more on top of each other, won't we?' snapped Runtling.

'Yes, but what if I'm on the bottom?'

'Then you'll come out flat! I suppose,' sighed Runtling, 'I suppose I'll have to be look-out, and not sleep.'

He sighed again. Being a leader was very tiring.

Fern got up. 'I'll take the second watch,' she said, very loudly and clearly. If Runtling was leader, Fern wished it to be known she was deputy leader.

It was not long before the sun rose. That only made things worse, for now they had to be quiet in case someone on the path heard them. They could either sleep – if that was possible – or lie awake feeling hungry, most painfully, unbearably, unspeakably hungry. It was going to be a long day.

Only a man and his dog came down the track that morning. The dog's keen nose picked up a smell of pig. He was inquisitive. Off he bounded along the trail which led to the barn.

Fern saw it first. 'Something's coming. A dog! It's a dog!'

In an instant the pigs were on their feet. Tail waving, the dog ran into the barn. He only wanted to play. But at the sight of those large, silent, staring pigs, his tail wagged more slowly and he turned his head uncertainly to look at a wall, so as to avoid their eyes. Then his master whistled for him. As though he were relieved, the dog swung round and bounded away.

The pigs waited in frozen silence. But nothing happened. Fern peered through the doorway. The path was empty. Man and dog had gone.

But unknown to the pigs something far more dangerous to them was going on this very morning. Two notices appeared on the roadside, one on the road past Taggerty's farm and the other outside the village of Pakton, where the post office and the pub and Kelly's Stores – the shop that sold everything were.

On both sides of each notice board was written in large black letters: POLICE WARNING – PIGS ON THE ROAD.

So the news was out after all. By midday almost everyone in the village knew that Taggerty's pigs had escaped. As they passed the news on to each other, people carefully arranged their faces to look serious, even aghast. But a picture kept entering their heads. A picture of Jos Taggerty red-faced, huffing and puffing up and down roads looking for his pigs, and it was impossible not to laugh.

'But poor old Taggerty! What a nuisance for him,'

they would say, to excuse their laughter.

'They can't be far away,' said the postman to Mr Kelly in the stores. 'Perhaps they've got into Jones's field and are digging up his turnips.'

They both started to grin. It was a pleasing thought. Mr Jones was not popular. But Mr Jones was keeping a sharp eye on his fields – just in case. So were other farmers – just in case.

At midday in the Holly Bush, the village pub, the first-comers were all talking about it. Ernie the postman, 'Sawdust' the carpenter, Old Bob his uncle, Johnny from Updown Farm, and Mary Mott his girlfriend.

'Pigs won't go far,' said Old Bob. 'Hunger'll get 'em. Then they're bound to go back to where their food is.'

'Yes,' added Johnny. 'You can lose a dog or a sheep, or a hen, but you can't lose twelve pigs. Not *twelve* pigs!'

'Of course not,' said Bessie, the pretty barmaid. 'Pigs are too big, and er … pink. There's no way twelve pigs could hide together without bits of them sticking out and being seen. No. Taggerty will find them before the day's out.'

'No, he won't,' called a loud voice from the door, and Tom Price, the cattle-truck driver, marched in. 'I've been at Taggerty's. I was supposed to take those pigs to market today but what did I find? Not a pig in sight and Taggerty lying in his bed with a face as white as a ghost.'

'Why, what's happened to him?' asked Bessie.

'Well…' Tom paused to make sure everyone was listening. 'Well, yesterday, near suppertime, it seems, Taggerty had the pigyard gate open. He was pushing in a bin of swill when the pigs suddenly took off and bolted through the gate. Well, Taggerty was in the way and he got knocked off his feet. He fell over … backwards … and hit his head, good and hard, on the concrete. He didn't get up. He just lay there, just lay there till Mrs T found him. And now he's in bed with concussion. They had the doctor, you know.'

'But what would frighten twelve pigs?' asked Bessie.

'Who knows? Mrs T, well, she talked about the devil entering the pigs, like in the Bible. A bit over-excited, I think she was.'

'More likely, they took fright at the smell of the swill,' said the postman, with a wink. 'Perhaps there was a rabbit in it, dead a month, or one of Taggerty's old socks. You know he never wastes anything.'

'We shouldn't joke about him really,' said Mary Mott, giggling.

'Well, anyway, what with these police warnings "PIGS ON THE ROAD" and all, we'll soon have news of them,' said Tom Price. 'No point in us all going on a pig hunt.'

The 'PIGS ON THE ROAD' sign was read by car drivers with surprise. They all went more slowly round the bends. Some who came from towns thought it would be rather jolly to meet pigs on the road and looked ahead hopefully. But they were to be disappointed. The pigs had long since turned off those roads and by now were far away.

CHAPTER 7

THE SECOND NIGHT

FERN STOOD ON WATCH at the empty doorway of the barn. It was raining. The puddle by the door got wider and deeper. The hours passed miserably. The rain dripped off her back and the puddle grew wider and wider, until there was no avoiding it.

Inside the barn the pigs were too hungry and frightened to sleep much. It was quite a relief when night fell and they could get up and go on again.

Heavy clouds blotted out the moon and they walked as though blind. They tripped and stumbled, and blinked the water from their eyes. If only they knew where they were going, they thought, or if only they could see where they were going. If only they could stop and eat. If only they hadn't come at all. And they were here, in all this, just because of what a cat had said ... Perhaps the cat had invented the whole story.

'Runtling,' Meadow and Breeze said, catching up with him. 'How do you know that cat wasn't making it all up, what she said?'

'If you were a half-starved cat and you were hot on

the trail of some rats that would feed you for several days, would you turn back just to tell a pig a story? The cat turned back to warn me because she hates the Taggertys. No, it was not a story.'

The pigs went on in silence 'till round the darkness of a clump of trees, a little way off, the blurred lights of a farmhouse came into view.

Runtling stopped. 'Keep away from that,' he warned. 'There'll be a dog. And it might not be chained up.'

Farm dogs – Taggerty's dog for example – they thought they owned the place, and sprang out and barked ridiculously at everyone passing by. If this happened late at night, the farmer would come out and look. Anyone prowling round at this time would be up to no good.

They had walked a long way round to avoid that farmhouse, at least the rain had almost stopped. By the light of a watery moon it was easier going, even on this rutted track. But they were plodding along more slowly than ever and tripping over small things.

We can't go much further without food, thought Runtling. He himself had begun to feel so weak that he didn't know whether his legs were carrying him, or if he was pulling them along after him.

From both sides of the rutted path rose the wet-earth smell of plough. Further on, though, came something else. It grew stronger. It was the powerful smell of brussels sprouts! Taggerty had sometimes chucked a sackful of overgrown stalky sprouts into the pigyard. There was always a scramble for them.

Young hedges bordered the sprouts field. The pigs nosed along the hedges looking for a gap to push through. Hidden in the tangle of weeds at the bottom of the hedge were curious things, a milk-bottle with dead leaves in it, one glove, a glass jar half-full of thick dark stuff, a small woollen hat – flat and muddy, and a dead rabbit. But they were too hungry to be curious about the rabbit.

'No crashing through the hedge just anywhere!' warned Runtling. 'We'll crawl through it, one at a time and in one and the same place. Then it'll look as though some boys had done it. So wait, Fern, and I'll find a place.'

On the field side of the hedge was a border of long grass, nettles and docks where tractors turned to make their next pass down the field.

'Runtling, perhaps we oughtn't to charge about the field trampling sprouts right and left. It'll be seen at once in the morning. If we stay on the grass borders and eat the sprouts alongside those it may not be seen for a day or two until someone comes into the field. By then we'd be far, far away,' suggested Fern.

'Let's do that,' said Runtling. 'Oh Fern, you're so sensible.'

The sprouts had been planted in rows. They were

young and tender, unlike Taggerty's. After half an hour the first row was almost gone. Hawthorn and Bramble were starting on the second row. Mist had found another dead rabbit and Meadow had found two.

That made four dead rabbits in the field. Four, Runtling noted. And the others said the rabbits seemed to be quite whole, not bitten or torn or anything. A niggling little fear crept into his mind. The rabbits ate sprouts and they died, and there wasn't a mark on them. We ate sprouts and… ?

CHAPTER 8

THE POISON FIELD

'MEADOW! MIST!' Runtling called anxiously. 'Show me the dead rabbits will you?'

Each rabbit lay near the bottom of the hedge. Round them the weeds and grass were flattened as though there had been a struggle.

'What do you make of that? Do you think it could have been a fox after them?'

'No, Runtling,' said Mist. 'I know what foxes do with their kill. Sow told us. She said they bury it quickly somewhere. Then another day when they're hungry, they come back and dig it up to eat. I don't know how they remember where it's hidden. But they do, foxes do.'

'Well...well...a large bird then?' suggested Runtling.

'A falcon? No, couldn't be. A falcon drops out of the sky straight down onto the rabbit, grips it in its talons and sweeps off. Off to some high secret place to eat it.' Mist shuddered at the thought.

'Some cats can catch rabbits, then they take them home to show off with,' laughed Meadow. 'But it can't

be a cat because the rabbits are still here. And it isn't a stoat because they kill and eat on the spot, and there's no smell of blood or bones about, is there?'

'How do you know all this?' Runtling asked, suddenly envious. 'You've spent all your lives in a pigsty too, so how can you know?'

'Sow used to tell us. Of course, she'd never actually seen any of it happen, but she'd heard about it from Old Sow. It's all in the Old Stories, and they're true, every one of them. I suppose you'd left home when Sow began to tell the Old Stories! Oh, well, it's a mystery, isn't it, how those rabbits died.' Mist and Meadow went back to the sprouts.

Runtling was left alone staring out across the field, that niggling little fear still there. What else could kill rabbits and leave no mark?

He was trying to remember something. He didn't have too many memories. So little had happened in that small sty, except for the rat. Ah, it must be hard for him now without the crumbs in the trough. They'd put rat poison down in the yard, and in the barn, and round the buildings. Rat had found four rats, dead, in the barn, and his sister, dead too, in the yard, and there wasn't a mark on any of them. 'It's how poison kills.' That's what the rat had said.

A sudden alarming thought occurred to Runtling. That must be how the rabbits had died. The field was poisoned! But surely the poison wouldn't be strong enough for large animals like pigs, when it was meant for small animals like rabbits?

The fear retreated a little, but it didn't vanish. It said: How are you feeling now, Runtling? Are you sure you're feeling all right? Quite sure?

Runtling stood and considered himself, bit by bit. First he concentrated on his feet, then his legs. How were they? They seemed to be as usual. On his body he spent longer. His tail still felt the same as usual, he thought. So did the middle of him, so did his head.

So far you're all right, Runtling, he thought to himself, but think about this. A pig is much bigger than a rabbit, so it might take much longer for the poison to begin working inside you. And that much longer before you start feeling odd ... then very odd ... then horrible ... then dead. And, what about the others?

Hurriedly Runtling crossed the field to the other pigs. Mist, Meadow, Leaf and Fern, and several others he could see, were lying down.

'Are you all right?' He tried to speak in an ordinary voice.

'Mmm...sleepy, just sleepy... over-eaten...' Fern murmured.

But the Piglings, Bramble and Hawthorn were still eating the sprouts.

'Stop eating!' he shrieked. 'Get out of here! Everyone get out of here. Now! Quick!'

Back on the track he began to explain. But he kept

his worst fears to himself. 'It could be that the poison was spread low down, near the ground where the rabbits eat, so we probably missed most of it. Anyway, the poison was for rabbits so it would be too weak for pigs. I'm all right, you can see, and no-one feels odd, do they?'

But the fear had followed him and, even as he spoke those comforting words, he thought: For all we know poison might strike suddenly. You're fine one moment and dead the next.

The rutted lane led to a pasture where cows were sleeping, and beyond that to fields and more fields. It was difficult finding their way in the dark, having to go through, under, over, round the field boundaries and gates. Up and down banks, always climbing higher, and now across a rocky stream 'where you can hardly see where to put your feet,' as Breeze remarked.

'I bet we haven't a clue where we are either, except it's somewhere different. It's not Taggerty land anyhow. It's much rougher and bumpier,' grumbled Hawthorn.

But at last they had climbed above the fields and their troublesome boundaries. On the short grass here they walked freely and laughed when startled sheep ran away in a panic. The poison scare was half forgotten. No-one felt the least bit ill. Only Runtling still looked a little grim.

It was still two hours before dawn when Hawthorn saw the road. 'Look down there,' he shouted. 'A wonderfully, totally empty road. Not a single farmhouse. We'll go fast on that. Let's go, Runtling. It's not too far down.'

It was an old road on one side of a valley. It ran through empty countryside until it disappeared into the far distance. As they trotted along, the pigs stared in wonder at the far side of the valley where the road rose up steeply into a long ridge of hills, quiet and steely in the moonlight.

'Is this the world?' they whispered.

Sometimes dark woodlands blotted out a hillside. On the top of one hill sat a curious black crown of trees, a round crown, not straggly like the other woods. It didn't look natural.

Nor was it. It was man-made long ago to entice foxes to live there. In this wood – this covert – the fox would find shelter, a bit of food, and somewhere to lie hidden, preferably in a roomy old hole in the ground between tree roots – its earth. The covert was there to make sure a fox or two could always be found nearby. Not for love of foxes, but for love of hunting foxes.

To the pigs it seemed an ideal place to spend the dangerous daylight hours, thick and dark and isolated. No road, nothing else near it.

Bramble looked hopefully at the covert. 'It'll be light soon. And the Piglings are tired. I don't know how much longer they can keep up.'

'Yes, Runtling. We must have walked twice as far tonight – because of the sprouts. Let's go there,' Breeze argued.

Runtling winced at the mention of sprouts, but he turned off the road to make for the covert.

It was further away than they had thought, and from the road they hadn't seen a ditch too broad for jumping, a bristling barbed-wire fence, and beyond it the long dew-drenched fields at the foot of the hill.

So it was already light when, muddy, scratched and torn, they began to plod up the steep hillside. The Piglings had dropped further and further behind. Bramble stayed with them to coax them on.

The rest were nearly at the top when a cry came from the Piglings: 'Wait! we can't go on! We can't go any further.'

Runtling turned to Fern. 'You take over the lead, will you? I'm going down to them.'

He found all three of them sprawled out on the rough grass. 'Having a nice rest, you three? I can see the headlines now, "Seen, lying on a hillside, three pink pigs shining brightly in the morning light!" All right! Sleep on a bit. I'll keep watch for you.'

Bramble looked grateful, and Runtling moved off a little way towards one of the hummocks dotted around the slopes. These were ant-hills, built up higher and higher by generations of white ants. Standing on one of these he would have a good view of the road and the valley they'd just left.

But the valley and road had entirely disappeared. Below, where the valley had been, lay a great bank of white cloud, through which peaked the upper slopes of hills rimmed with light. Lost in wonder and amazement at this sight, Runtling forgot why he was there.

A whole cloud has fallen into the valley, thought Runtling. It must be a cloud, but it looks woolly and thick. So thick you could walk on it.

He imagined running down the hill and jumping onto the cloud. It was soft and springy, and he laughed and rolled and plunged about in the mist and cool of it. Then he lay floating on his back, swaying gently under a great sky where higher clouds drifted. Then he thought he would run along the cloud to the very end of it and look over the edge. To get up he had only to roll over and tread lightly.

'Runtling!' someone was calling, 'Runtling!' and he found he was back on the hummock again. The Piglings were awake and Fern was calling out, 'Runtling. What's delaying you? You can be seen out there in the open. Come on into the covert!'

The three pigs followed slowly behind Runtling, up the hill. The rest were already in the covert. Hawthorn and Fern were waiting for them just below it. They too were staring at that cloud and the land spreading on and on beyond it.

Fern said, puzzled, 'It's strange. I can't see where the world ends. Can you?'

A little wind ruffled the leaves in the wood above them and wafted down a scent, a scent that spoke strongly of food...

As the pigs were making their way into the covert, a boy carrying a sack entered the sprouts field. He noticed that the first two rows of sprouts had gone and that there was a lot of trampling round the borders of the field. He wondered. If it had been animals, now, they would have been all over the field. Maybe it was someone after their sprouts. Dad would be mad, hopping mad. But breakfast was waiting, and first he must get the rabbits.

He bent down to the snare and carefully released the loop of thin copper wire round the rabbit's neck. The rabbit had made frantic efforts to get free of the capturing wire but this had only pulled the loop tighter and tighter round its neck until it was dead. He put the dead rabbit in the sack and reset the snare ready for the night, then checked the other snares. Only four rabbits caught. Not as many as usual. Perhaps they'd been afraid to enter the field because of whoever had been there. Dad would be hopping mad.

CHAPTER 9

THE HUNT

ALL THROUGH THE WOOD came the sound of the pigs' heavy bodies crashing excitedly about in the under-growth, the sound of twigs snapping, of crunching and gobbling. They forgot about the secrecy and silence of an escape. They forgot about Taggerty. They thought only about the enticing smells that rose up from the woodland floor, the same sort of food smells that had tantalised them on those long hungry journeys of the last two nights.

All this was very unwelcome to two large crows who had adopted the wood. They awoke in a fright and scolded the pigs from the safety of the treetops, flapping and cawing dementedly.

The pigs ignored them. They had just discovered the joys of rootling – digging about with their snouts in the leaf-mould and the soft black earth of the woodland floor. Down there they found food, food they'd never tasted before – pale tender roots, long tap roots and the sweet sticky bulbs of bluebells, hundreds of them. And there were beetles to be snapped up, grubs, wood lice and slithery writhing worms. Any hard woody roots lying in their way, were torn up and tossed away.

The rootling continued. When a sudden extraordinary sound rent the air, the pigs took little notice. But Meadow, the lookout pig, heard it. He was rootling on the very edge of the covert and had a view of the valley below. The unearthly sound startled him.

He lifted his head and pricked up his ears, listening. It sounded again. A triumphant brassy blare – Tarantara! Tarantara! It flashed fearfully through Meadow's mind that it could be saying 'Hurrah! Hurrah! Here the pigs are, they are'.

He hid behind a bush. He could still peer out down the valley without being seen. Below, in the distance, he could see men in pink coats on horseback following a pack of foxhounds.

The leading hounds ran, tail up, nose down to the ground, following a scent. For two hours they had been following this scent, losing, then finding it again. It was the scent of a fox on the run, and it would lead them like a pathway to where they would find him. Then they would have it. Sink their teeth in it, shake it like a stick. Fight each other for bits of it.

But Meadow knew nothing of this. To him it could only be the pig hunt they all feared, only more awful, much more awful. Not in their worst imaginings had there been a pack of dogs and men on horseback. Meadow fled back into the wood.

'Stop! … Stop munching!' he yelled. 'Hide! They're

coming … A pack of dogs … Men on horseback. Men specially dressed up for it too.'

'Where? Where are they?' Runtling shouted.

'Down in the valley…Heading this way.'

The pigs pushed and crammed themselves under bushes and low boughs. Stiff with fear, they crouched there with closed eyes.

A fox, fur matted with sweat, tail dragging with exhaustion, turned up the hill towards the covert. There he'd go to earth, and he'd stand to fight if needs be, just where his earth's dark interior narrowed and tunnelled between tree roots and the hard-banked soil. There he'd fight … his last fight?

The fox was halfway up the hill. He caught the strong whiff of pig. He veered towards it, knowing that the scent of pig was stronger than the scent of fox. He cast around for where the smell was thickest.

It will smother my scent, he thought.

He reached the covert and made for a large hole between the roots of an old beech tree. He disappeared into it.

The foxhounds were rounding the foot of the hill, baying and yelping with excitement, for the scent was strong and fresh. The pigs heard them and crouched lower. The fox heard them and pressed against the far side of the earth, waiting in suspense. But in his eyes was a sly, even cocky look.

Halfway up the hill the hounds stopped, puzzled. The

scent of fox had given way to a strong scent of pig. This was of no interest to them. They had grown up among farm animals. If they had dared to chase any they would have been whipped.

They ran here and there, frustrated, then appeared to give up. They were tired anyway. Some lay down. The riders reined in and waited below. In the end, they called the hounds off, turned back along the valley and jogged slowly homewards.

CHAPTER 10

ANGER IN THE WOOD

A BRIEF SILENCE FELL in the wood. The two crows flew down. They pecked energetically at the upturned earth, finding an unusual number of insects and other goodies. They were still at it when the pigs, rather subdued, crept out of hiding. The hunt had been a shock.

The crows were now even angrier with the pigs, for this time they were interrupting their feeding. They started cawing and flapping again, taking large hops towards the pigs. The pigs grew nervous.

'This is our wood,' cawed the crows. 'You've no right here. You're in our way. We're feeding ... feeding ...'

Runtling said quickly, 'It's just a short visit. We'll be gone by dark.'

But Fern was bolder. 'And who provided you with this feast anyway? Who turned over the soil so that you could get all those creepy-crawlies? We did!'

The crows cocked their heads to one side and considered this. Finally, they replied, 'We have agreed that you may stay here and continue digging – as it's

only temporary. And, may we ask, where are you off to this evening?'

'We won't know 'till we arrive,' sighed Runtling.

'That's not much of an answer.'

'Well, the truth is we're running away from Taggerty's, and we must take the shortest route to get as far away from him as quickly as possible.'

'Ah, yes, Taggerty's! We've been over Taggerty's, but not often. He has a gun. He shot my cousin. We'd be most happy to help you escape him.'

'You must do this,' continued one crow. 'Look where the sun sets. Due west. Go due west. That's the opposite direction to Taggerty's. He's due east. And the shortest way is always the straightest way. It's the way we take. So go as straight as a crow flies, and don't meander round.'

'But what happens if due west leads straight through a village?'

'Then tip-toe through the village. Of course, we would just fly over.'

'Thirteen pigs tip-toeing through a village!' The pigs fell over laughing at the idea. 'Pigs can't tip-toe!'

'Stop,' squawked the crow. 'The only village due west is twenty miles away. There's a tall church spire in the middle of it. No distance by air. An easy flight. But overland ... well... that's a matter you'd know more about. Don't envy you though. Four legs – quite a handicap – always earthbound. Better off with a couple of legs and a pair of wings, like us. Move anywhere, anytime. Distance no object.'

'And by the way,' chipped in the other crow, 'that's not the only village hereabouts. There's a nearer village northwest, and another northeast. No, to be exact, it's east northeast.'

'Wrong again!' interrupted the first crow. 'It's north northeast.'

The second crow hopped in annoyance. 'Ignore that. I repeat. East northeast. Not that it matters, for both are off course. But should you approach either village, reverse! You are travelling in the wrong direction. Remember head west towards the setting sun. Then navigate by the stars. You'll find it easy, quite easy really. Well. Bon voyage!'

I've heard that before too, thought Runtling. 'Easy' means it's difficult, or impossible. Let's hope it's only difficult.

The fox slept deeply. It was afternoon before he came out from the earth. He looked around his covert, dismayed. There were thirteen pigs digging it up. He rushed at them, barking harshly.

'This is my covert. This is where I live. Look what a filthy mess you've made of it. What are you doing here anyway? You're trespassing. Now clear off. Go!'

What could the pigs say? Go they couldn't, wouldn't. It was still broad daylight.

Runtling stepped forward. 'I'm very sorry. We had no idea … I'll explain …'

And he told the fox their whole story right from the beginning. In spite of himself, the fox grew more and more interested and sympathetic. His own life was pretty dramatic too from time to time.

'But, about the poisoned sprouts,' said the fox thoughtfully, 'it's unbelievable that a farmer would sprinkle, or maybe paint, each sprout with poison. Hundreds – thousands – of sprouts! Think of the time. Think of the cost. No, it's my belief those rabbits were snared. Nearly every farmer keeps snares. They're cheap. And they're deadly. They set snares for foxes too. There's little I don't know about snares. Of course you pigs haven't the eyes to see snares at night, especially among leaves and grass.'

The pigs looked at Runtling. He turned his head in embarrassment and looked away. He had got it completely wrong!

Then the fox told them all that had happened in the hunt, of his clever idea of diving into the thick of their pig smell, of staying in it 'till he reached his earth, and of how it threw the hounds off his scent. So the rest of the day passed happily. The fox told breathless tales of the hunt, and the pigs told stories of the farmyard and humans.

And now it was dusk and time for the fox to become the hunter rather than the hunted. The first rabbits would be out, and he was hungry.

'And you'll be leaving very soon too,' he reminded the pigs. 'You know what lies due west. The moon is rising, so you'll be able to see to find your way. As for the covert, well, I suppose it'll grow over again one day and I admit that having you here saved my life!'

They were all a little sorry to part.

CHAPTER 11

THEY CAME TO A RIVER

THIS WAS THE THIRD NIGHT of the great escape and the pigs were tired and hungry again.

'I'm not used to all this trotting. Trotting ... trotting ... trotting. Trotting all night and every night.'

'Neither am I. My hooves are wearing thin.'

'Why do we always have to go through brambles instead of around them?'

'My left ear is hurting.'

'My left leg is, and that's worse.'

They kept on asking Runtling, 'How far have we got to go now? Are we nearly there? How much further is it?'

'No idea. Not the slightest idea yet,' Runtling confessed.

'Don't you know where we are then?' they asked him.

'Not that either.'

One of the Piglings was weeping. 'We're lost. Hopelessly lost.'

'Are we, at least, going in the right direction?'

'Well,' said Runtling. 'The crow said "Go straight

as the crow flies". Straight means straight on.'

'Oh, straight on again!' they groaned. 'Going straight on is so awful. Why can't we go round things instead of always straight over things or straight under things or straight through things? Things which hurt too. Hawthorn hedges. Barbed wire. Squeezing through gates.'

Runtling tried to explain. 'I'm only making sure we go straight like the crow said. If we went round things that turn corners, like hedges, we could lose our direction. We could find we were going a roundabout way back towards Taggerty's. Anyway the next bit looks all right. And it's downhill. Cheer up.'

At the bottom of the slope their way was suddenly barred. Hidden by the trees that overhung it was a river. The pigs stood on its banks, staring at the dark water. Now all that the pigs had ever seen of water was a large puddle in the pigyard. It was always there for a day or two after a lot of rain. It was cool and splashy and nice.

They were puzzled. 'This is a very large puddle.'

'And it seems to have no end either way,' said Bramble.

'But, look, you can just see more trees there. That must be the other side.'

'Well,' said Runtling, 'straight on means straight across this water, doesn't it? It'll be nice! Come on ... let's go.'

It was exciting. All crowded together, pushing and splashing, they rushed in.

But this was not like the puddle in the pigyard. 'The water's coming up to the top of my legs,' called out Meadow from the front. 'Better than the puddle in the yard!'

But he spoke too soon. A step or two further in and he was no longer sure that water was fun. 'It's splashing over my sides now.' This was frightening.

'There's too much water here,' screamed a Pigling.

Then the water closed over their backs and they were straining their necks to keep their heads above it. The water was pulling at them, trying to carry them along with it as it flowed past into empty darkness. In a panic they fought the water with pounding legs. Striking legs. Fast, faster and faster. Keeping their heads up. Keeping their heads above the water to get to safety, the safety of the other bank.

And they found they were actually running in the water — running, without their feet touching the bottom. For this running was a swimming, in the kind of way all four-legged animals swim.

At last, one by one, the pigs reached the other bank. Panting, excited, they scrambled up it.

'That was marvellous!' said Mist.

'It was terrible!' said the Piglings with one voice.

'Well, terribly marvellous then!' said Runtling as he bounced ahead, all clean and fresh.

CHAPTER 12

TELL-TALE HOOF PRINTS

EARLY NEXT MORNING a fox strolled along the river bank. Suddenly he stopped and wrinkled his nose in disgust.

Pig! The smell is unmistakable and awful. About an hour old, I'd guess. And there must have been many more than one pig. Could it be that lot who messed up my covert? My friends, the runaways? Then they've come a remarkable distance in a short time. Well, for pigs, that is.

The fox studied the soft earth and mud on the bank. Idiots! Just look at all those hoof prints. They should have jumped from grass into the river. And they should have spread out instead of taking off together, and taking off from mud too. They might just as well have put up a notice to help everyone who's looking for them:

> We were right here.
> Now cross the river
> to find more signs.
> Love,
> The Pigs.

Oh Pink and Hairless Ones, who know not the ways of the wild, I will yet save you from your folly, he intoned.

The fox then rose on his hind legs and began a strange jumping, stamping dance exactly on top of their hoofprints. When he had finished, the ground was churned up as though a great fight had taken place on the bank, but between what sort of animals it would be hard to say.

I think I'll check on where the pigs are lying up, the fox thought.

He swam the river with ease, shook himself dry

and, nose to the ground, trotted off. He would hunt on the way. He was in no hurry, not yet.

This same morning, after she had settled Mr Taggerty comfortably on the sofa, Mrs Taggerty got the van out to look for the pigs. The village had been wrong. The pigs had not come home for food. And believe it or not, it was possible to lose twelve pigs.

Mrs Taggerty called at farmhouses. She dropped in at pubs. She leaned over gates and asked tractor drivers. Nobody had seen them. But everybody declared they would watch out for them.

It was lucky for the pigs that people had lost the habit of walking any distance more than about a mile. Long ago, before cars were on the road, country people walked everywhere. There was time then to notice the many little things they passed even when taking shortcuts along the tracks and footpaths and fields. Certainly to notice the footprints of thirteen pigs. And in those days this story would have ended there.

CHAPTER 13

HOPELESS FARM

IT WAS DANGEROUSLY CLOSE to daybreak. Still the pigs had found no sort of cover. They were in a lane with a stone wall on the right, too high to climb, and a thick brambly hedge with one or two old trees sticking out of it on the left.

What was behind that thick hedge they wondered? Well, somewhere there must be a gate they could look through. Further on they found it, a heavy old wooden gate. Fastened, chained up and padlocked, with bars too close together to squeeze through.

Leaning crookedly on the gate-post was a large notice. It looked as though it had been there for a long time. It read 'FOR SALE : HOPE FARM – TWENTY-FIVE ACRES' Some-one had added the 'LESS' after 'HOPE', so that the sign read: 'FOR SALE: HOPELESS FARM'.

And hopeless it was. The last farmer who had owned Hope Farm had grown too old to work the land. He sold off his cows, and sat in front of the fire all day. He let the fields do as they pleased. He could no longer be bothered.

The grass grew very long, bent over, and yellowed.
The weeds grew stronger and invaded the fields and
with every year they had become taller and more
numerous.

The pigs were delighted with what they saw – a
field full of nettles and thistles and docks, gorse too.
Bracken was growing head high and thick on a bank
above a stream. Beyond that field was another field
and another, all in the same state.

'It's marvellous.'

'Just look at it all!'

'Look at that bracken cover. There's enough food
there for a year. But how do we get in?' Runtling
asked.

'Through the hedge?'

'But it's all blackthorn here.' Even pigs avoid blackthorn's long needles that stick in flesh and cause swellings.

'It may be hawthorn further down the road. That's not so bad,' suggested Fern.

And they turned to look for a less damaging kind of bush to push through.

Through the sleepy, silent dawn came a distant sound – the dig-dig-dag of a tractor starting up.

'Ssh! Ssh! Listen!' hissed Runtling. 'A tractor! Through the hedge. Quickly!'

Runtling had no choice. What was he leader for? He lowered his head, half-closed his eyes and pushed and thrust into the blackthorn hedge taking the needles in his own flesh. Through the gap he made, the others followed. They streamed through the first field and through a gap into the second field.

There, waiting for them, was another large thicket of blackthorn. The bushes grew in a circle which had not quite closed up. Animals had used it long ago for shelter. Their constant treading had kept the way in open, and had kept its grassy centre flattened. The pigs flung themselves down on the soft centre. The tractor passed down the road. The driver saw nothing. As the sound of the engine faded away, the pigs, too tired to move, fell asleep in a heap where they lay.

And there the fox found them.

'Nice place you've got here,' he remarked.

The pigs slept on.

He looked them over. 'You're even thinner than you were two days ago. Lost a lot of weight trotting every night, haven't you? You have length, and you have height, but no width. Your sides are flat! Well,' he said, as no-one was sufficiently awake to answer him, 'I'll take a stroll round the new estate.'

They were still asleep when he returned.

'I think you'll be around here for a long time, and that suits me. Ah Runtling!' the fox nudged him awake. 'Runtling. There's a house on your estate. It's deserted. Invite me there for dinner one day. Make it chicken – head and all – underdone. And, by the way, go easy on the bracken.' Runtling blinked, nodded and fell asleep again.

CHAPTER 14

A LAND FIT FOR PIGS

IT WAS AFTERNOON when the pigs woke. One by one they stole away from the thicket. Now this was against the rules. For they had agreed that, while they were escaping, no pig should leave cover until dark. But their hunger wouldn't wait until night.

'And what about that bracken?' they said. 'Isn't that cover enough? It's a good two pigs high, or higher.'

The bracken was indeed a forest of food where they could disappear from sight. Only the bracken tops waved rather oddly as the pigs snatched at the lower fronds.

They were still eating at half-past four when the tractor driver turned home for his tea. From his high tractor seat he could see fairly well over the roadside hedges, and he happened to notice those oddly waving bracken tops, and wondered ... But he didn't investigate. He wanted his tea.

Over tea he said, 'There are badgers at Hopeless. Saw them, rolling in the bracken.'

'I'll have them if they roll in my corn,' replied his father and added, 'I suppose the Faraways will be jumping for joy when they find they've got badgers on their land. You know they asked me was there any wildlife around here before they bought that place. Wildlife here? Not on my farm, thank you! They didn't like that. "Well, it's got as much right to live here as you or I have," they said, and walked off.

'They're weird, just weird, those Faraways. With her long hair and dingle-dangle bangles. And him with his beard and sandals. Ridiculous!'

'I know,' said the son. 'They say one or two of that sort are trying to move in around here. Trying to buy up small farms with poor land, going cheap. The Faraways are moving into Hopeless in two weeks' time. Did you know?'

'But there's nothing growing there. Nothing but weeds! The land's only fit for pigs! They'll never get rid of those weeds. Not unless they plough it, and grow potatoes for two years. To me, they don't look as though they've got the money for that.'

He remembered the battered old van they'd arrived in, repainted a horrible bright blue.

And it was true. The Faraways didn't have the money for that.

In Hopeless the bracken had quietened down. Meadow had just left it.

'I'm sick of bracken,' he gulped, making for the stream.

Some of the others were already there, looking pale.

'I feel awful,' moaned Meadow.

'You'll feel better when you've been sick,' the others told him.

'Why, have you been sick?'

'Yes. All of us. We're going for a lie-down in the thicket.'

Meadow stayed by the stream. He tried not to be sick. He didn't want to be sick. He was afraid of being sick. Then, he saw Runtling coming slowly out of the bracken. He wasn't looking very cheerful either. And he was muttering, 'I feel rather ill – and you look ill too.'

'You'll be better when you've been sick,' Meadow told him. Suddenly he turned his back and surrendered helplessly to being sick. A moment later, Runtling did the same.

After a short drink in the stream, they wandered back to the thicket where the rest were lying.

'We've got to have a meeting. Now,' Runtling announced, 'there's something I forgot to tell you.'

The pigs raised their heads weakly.

'This morning the fox came when we were all asleep. He said to go easy on the bracken, but I wasn't properly awake so I forgot. Now we know what he meant. We'll have to have another rule. About bracken. So, from now on, we rootle for our food till evening, then have a fresh bracken supper.'

'There could be another new rule,' added Hawthorn daringly. 'No trotting after dark!'

'That would mean we stay here!'

'And sleep in the thicket every night!'

They looked at Runtling.

'Well!' said Runtling. 'It looks as though no-one owns this place. Doesn't it remind you of the world Sow talked about, you remember, where nuts fall from trees and pigs are free. Perhaps this is it? Let's stay here.'

That night they felt safe at last, and slept long and deep in the dark still thicket.

In the days that followed, they rootled from morning to evening. Under the beech-tree by the house they found beech-nuts. They were delicious. Acorns too, under the oak tree, which the pigs cracked open and ate noisily. There was no-one to hear them. They turned up the soil and overturned the weeds. They ate the grass and trampled it. Gradually the fields of Hopeless Farm began to change colour from green to earth brown.

CHAPTER 15

NICK AND POLLY

ON A BRIGHT AUTUMN DAY, a van pulled up at the gate of Hopeless Farm. It was a battered old van, repainted a vivid blue, a blue even brighter and bluer than the sky that day. On the top of the van and inside it were mountains of luggage, bulging sacks, pans, rolls of bedding and boxes of crockery which had rattled all through the journey. Disentangling their feet from the bottom layer of packing, out got the new farmers of Hopeless, Nick and Polly Faraway.

They did not look in the least like farmers, and most certainly not like the Taggertys. The Faraways were young and straight and tall and slim. And what farmers wear beards and spectacles and a great mane of dark hair like Nick? And do ordinary farm women run about in bare legs with bangles jingling on their arms, and do they look as gentle and happy as Polly? Well, not many, not for long. They are all too busy.

Nick and Polly didn't seem to bother greatly about their clothes. Nick wore a large and baggy pullover in bright green and red, hand-knitted, not very well, by Polly. It was a bit torn at the bottom too. And Polly wore some sort of loose white top. Printed on it was 'SAVE THE TREES' with a picture of trees above.

They opened the gate and stood on the pathway for a moment in silence. There was their castle, a stone farmhouse among trees, and around it stretched their kingdom. Within this kingdom lay many things, trees, banks, tangles of hazel and hawthorn, a stream – a rushy stream– and a hidden glade in a blackthorn thicket. It was hard to believe that this was all theirs, every tree and leaf, theirs.

'Polly! Polly! ' cried Nick. But Polly's eyes were fixed on the castle.

'Polly, look! Something's happened to the land. It's been dug up. And look there are pigs there!'

Polly looked. 'Oh no... Oh!... It's been ruined. Who let pigs in? It's been ruined! What a mess! What a ghastly rotten mess!'

The pigs saw them coming and made a rush for the blackthorn thicket.

'Polly, a lot of the weeds have gone.'

'But a lot of the grass has too.'

'Well, that wasn't much good, that rank old grass. Don't you see? The pigs have been ploughing up the land for us. And fertilising it too. Pig dung's marvellous stuff. Things grow like mad in it. If the pigs stay long enough to finish digging, we can start growing our own vegetables.'

'And oats for our porridge, and wheat for flour so

we can make our own bread,' added Polly. 'What a dream!'

When they reached the thicket the pigs were bunched together close up against the blackthorn, staring at them. They looked like wild pigs, thin and sharp-eyed.

Nick and Polly stared back. With the pigs living there it seemed like a real farm already. Both stood quite still, afraid that a sudden movement might alarm the pigs. Polly was thinking that if she and Nick were no bigger than pigs, they would be less frightening to them. She sank down on her knees, and Nick knelt down too, slowly and carefully.

He held out a hand and made small grunting noises. One or two pairs of ears moved perplexedly. Polly held out her hand and talked to them in a sweet, whispery voice.

'Piggywigs ... Piggywigs ... Piggy-wiggy-wiggy-wigs. Here piggywigs, wiggy-wigs.' The pigs shifted about uneasily.

'Let's try them with food,' suggested Polly. 'We've got those loaves in the van.'

They rose slowly and backed away. The pigs turned to each other anxiously,

'What are they doing here? This is our land now.'

'But what are they? Are they real people?'

People were dangerous. The only ones the pigs knew were the Taggertys and one or two others who called into the farm. And they all had loud voices, not soft, coaxing voices like Nick and Polly. Runtling remembered Mr Stubbs too, with an old cap on his head which he never took off, whatever the weather. He could hear Mr Stubbs even now, how he shouted and swore at his dogs.

Nick and Polly came back with two loaves. They tore them into pieces and laid the pieces down in lines. Close to the last line, they sat and waited. But the pigs would only eat the bread farthest away.

'I wish they could understand that we want to be their friends, that we wouldn't harm them,' said Polly sadly.

'Hm ... they will ... in time. They seem very suspicious, very suspicious of people. I wonder why,' replied Nick.

'Well, let's go and unpack the van, and leave them to think it over.'

CHAPTER 16

PIGS PLOUGHMEN

IT SEEMED SAFE to come out of the thicket now. The pigs were glad it was daytime so no-one could possibly suggest escaping. They didn't want to escape. This was their home now. If anyone had to go, it should be those two with the bread.

'You know,' said Runtling, 'I think they're trying to please us. They even seem a bit afraid of us. Well ... it wouldn't take four of us to knock them down, would it? If we had to, I mean. Maybe we'll be the bosses here.'

That evening the Faraways sat by the fire in the old stone farmhouse wondering where the pigs had come from.

'They must have been here for days and days. Their owners don't seem much bothered about them, do they? Perhaps they'll let them stay until they've finished ploughing up our land,' said Nick hopefully.

'I wish they could be ours. Cows and sheep are fine, but they are so, so ... aloof! Pigs aren't. You can always see what they're feeling.'

'The trouble is,' said Nick, 'if we had pigs we'd get

too fond of them and never be able to sell them off. Unless,' he added, 'we found them a job for life. Wait, I know – ploughing! That's it! Pigs can be used to plough. I remember I once saw pigs on an organic farm digging up a field. They really churned it up. The farmer said pigs were better than tractors, and cheaper. And it got the pig dung on the land without the cost of spreading it. And got rid of all the weeds too without using poisons. Poison can kill more than the weeds, you know.

'We could start by hiring pigs out for a fee to farmers to plough up their small fields and their rough land, where there's only bracken and gorse and stuff, like parts of Hopeless.'

'Oh Nick, I like those parts of Hopeless. They're exciting, and they're home for other creatures too, wild ones.'

'But wildlife doesn't eat bracken, Polly. That's why there's so much of it. You should tell the pigs to get rid of the bracken and save the rest! You seem to be learning to grunt quite well.

'And Polly, remember there's poor land, rough land which is not supposed to be worth the cost of ploughing up and sowing with grass. Pigs could work miracles there!'

'I'll bet the farmers won't believe us. They'll just think we're a couple of starry-eyed crackpots.'

'But,' said Nick, 'they'll have to believe it. We'll

invite them to Hope Farm to see for themselves.'

'Hope Farm, The Pigs Ploughman Demonstration Farm.' They were both getting excited by the idea.

'We'll advertise in the paper and put notices in shop windows.'

'And paint out the "less" in Hopeless to start with.'

'And become friends with the pigs.'

'And find out whose pigs they are. And buy them.'

'But where's the money to come from?'

Silence followed.

Then Polly said slowly, 'I suppose I could sell that gold necklace of my Auntie May's. What's the use of something so valuable that you daren't wear it for fear of losing it? Something you have to hide away in a safe place. Anyway I'd never wear it here. Real rubies. Real gold. But it might be enough to buy thirteen pigs.'

CHAPTER 17

AT MRS DEW'S

THE NEXT MORNING, Polly and Nick set out for Coxton village shop.

'We'll need more bread for the pigs – and a sack of potatoes. They look so thin. And we ought to find out where we can get sacks of proper pigmeal,' said Polly.

'But,' warned Nick, 'don't ask anyone round here. We don't want anyone to know – not just yet – that we're looking after thirteen stray pigs. Some busybody might start interfering.'

Above the shop window hung an old sign 'Dew Provisions'. Mrs Dew was inside – rosy-faced, plump, and inquisitive.

'Hello,' said the Faraways as they entered. 'We're Nick and Polly Faraway. We've just taken over Hope Farm.'

'Oh really! I am pleased to meet you. I'm Mrs Dew.'

'How do you do, Mrs Dew. Could you spare three large wholemeal loaves and, if you've got one, a sack of potatoes, please?'

'Oh, so you've got a family, have you?' enquired Mrs Dew.

Nick nudged Polly, warningly.

'No, no, there's just us,' Polly replied. 'We're vegetarians, you see, so we eat a lot of bread and potatoes. And we ... er ... feed the birds too, you know.'

'Being out of doors a lot gives us huge appetites,' added Nick. 'Would you save us three loaves for tomorrow, too?'

'Why, of course.'

Three loaves for Mrs Faraway, she noted in her order book.

'Thanks Mrs Dew. Bye.'

Mrs Dew was curious. Such quantities of bread and potatoes, just for two? Impossible! Who else is living there? One or two they don't want to mention? Someone wanted by the police? No. Couldn't be. But they certainly do look odd, those two. Though not bad.

The Faraways went home, laughing. 'How dew dew, Mrs Dew! How dew dew, Mrs Dew,' they chanted.

Back on the farm, they took two loaves of bread to the pigs. The pigs were bolder today and snatched the bread from wherever it fell. Nick was so encouraged by this that he spent the whole afternoon making a long wooden trough for them, long enough for each pig to have its own place. And Polly drove off to find pigmeal and buckets.

The next day they filled buckets with boiled potatoes and pigmeal, trundled them along in a wheelbarrow, then poured the good thick mixture into the trough. They stood a little way off and waited.

When the smell of a really good swill reached the pigs, they came running. They ate until not a crumb, hardly a smear remained.

At the same time the following day, came the sound of the wheelbarrow and the aroma of food. Within a minute thirteen enthusiastic pigs were escorting the wheelbarrow and Nick and Polly to the trough.

Meadow followed close by Polly's legs. Polly reached down and rubbed his back. Meadow ignored her. His thoughts were entirely on pigmeal and potatoes. But he didn't avoid Polly's hand either. And while the pigs were eating, Polly scratched quite a few more backs.

'We're winning, Nick! We're winning!' she said triumphantly.

Not many days later, they could walk up to almost any pig, give it a friendly slap, or scratch its back. Sometimes the pig would grunt with pleasure and arch its back for more.

They knew they should start to look for the pigs' owner, but they kept putting it off – suppose the owner wouldn't sell or suppose the price was more than the gold necklace was worth?

'But,' said Nick one day, 'suppose the owner arrived while we were out and just loaded the pigs into a truck and took them away – who knows where?'

Polly was alarmed. 'You stay here and guard the pigs. I'm going to Mrs Dew's.'

'Mrs Dew,' Polly said breathlessly, 'there are thirteen pigs on Hope Farm. Do you know of anyone round here who might have lost them?'

'Well, now … I haven't heard,' said Mrs Dew slowly. 'But I'll ask Tom.'

Tom Dew worked at the garage but he came home at mid-day for a meal.

'Tom!' called Mrs Dew.

Tom came in wiping his mouth.

'Tom. Has anyone round here lost any pigs that you've heard of?'

'Not that I've heard. And I'd be bound to have heard if they had! How long have you had them?'

'Oh, about a week or so. You see we've been expecting the owner to call every day. If you suddenly lost all those pigs, you'd call round all the local farms looking for them wouldn't you? We couldn't turn them out on to the road, could we?'

'Very good of you, Mrs Faraway. I would charge the owner for their keep if I were you. But it seems those pigs must have come a distance. There's no-one keeping pigs round Coxton. But they do Oldcastle way, I've heard.'

'Oldcastle! Too far away. They'd never get here from Oldcastle. Think, Tom, think,' commanded Mrs Dew.

'I *am* thinking … Now I do recall – but it was a while ago – some talk of pigs that escaped from somewhere Oldcastle way. I heard there were police warnings on the roadsides there, saying "PIGS ON THE ROAD". We got a bit of a laugh out of that. Maybe, maybe they're the pigs on your land. Why not ring Oldcastle police? Telephone box is round the corner.'

CHAPTER 18

FOR EVER AND EVER

MRS TAGGERTY answered her telephone.

'What! Where?... Where did you say they were? Thank you. We'll be along there as soon as possible.'

'The pigs have been found,' she cried out to Taggerty. 'The police say they're at Hope Farm in Coxton, wherever that is. Isn't it Haxham way? But that must be thirty miles away. I can't believe it!'

'Well, you go,' growled Taggerty. 'Arrange to meet Timpson there with his truck. See that he gives you a price for the pigs straight off the field. So he's got to load them. Heaven help him! Get the price up as much as you can of course, but don't come home without selling them.'

Mr Timpson and the Faraways were waiting near the gate for Mrs Taggerty's arrival. The Faraways looked nervous, even more so when Mrs Taggerty got out of her car.

'Mrs Taggerty,' said Mr Timpson. 'There are thirteen pigs here, not twelve.'

Mrs Taggerty's face fell. Not their pigs? Oh don't be so daft, she told herself. Twelve or thirteen, their pigs or not their pigs, better those than none.

'Take a look, Mrs Taggerty. Are they yours? You can see three of them just there.'

The three pigs were by the stony track that led from the gate to the farmhouse. They were grazing a new and most tender growth of grass along its edges. Now and then came a quiet grunt of contentment.

'Oh yes, that's them,' Mrs Taggerty said. 'Well, well, who would have thought to find them here.'

Instantly the pigs raised their heads. That voice! That voice! Mrs Taggerty's voice! And then they saw her staring at them over the gate. So they'd been found. After all that, they'd been found. Mrs Taggerty. The man. The cattle truck. The nightmare. All the horror was back. But this time it was real, it was actually happening... now. They'd be put in the truck and driven off to ... to be ... The pigs fled.

There was no time to think or plan. Only to get away. Which way? Runtling, all of them, rushed headlong for the gap they had forced in the blackthorn hedge many days past.

'It's blocked,' yelled Runtling.

Only three days before Nick had blocked it firmly to keep out stray sheep or dogs. He didn't want any farmer on his land collecting stray animals for fear he'd see the pigs.

'We can't get through,' Fern shouted.

'Well push through somewhere else. Anywhere.

Hurry! Hurry!'

'But it's thick blackthorn and a fence now too. It's hopeless. It'll take hours to get through.'

'And it's daytime and we'll be seen,' wept the Piglings. 'They'll follow us.'

So they were trapped, were they? Runtling's fear turned to anger, then to hate. And his words came slow and cold.

'I'm not going. I'm staying. We must fight. Who will fight with me? We are thirteen, they're only three. Even if more come, remember our bite. It'll cripple them. Come on, wait for them in the thicket ... our fortress ... Do you trust me?'

They had no choice.

'Yes, these pigs are ours all right,' Mrs Taggerty said, although she hardly recognised them. 'But they look much thinner. Of course they've lost a lot of weight. Been short of food all those days. Must have been.'

'That's just it, Mrs Taggerty,' Mr Timpson was apologetic but firm. 'I'm afraid I can't take them. I only deal in fat pigs. My trade is with butchers, you see. I wish I could help, but I don't know of anyone looking for pigs to fatten at the moment.'

Polly stepped forward quickly.

'Mr Timpson, we would take the pigs if we could. But we've just bought this farm. It cost us every penny we had so we can't pay cash. But I have a gold neck-

lace. I haven't had time to have it valued. Mrs Taggerty, would you be interested in that?'

Mr Timpson glanced kindly at Polly.

'May I be permitted to see it, Mrs Faraway? I may be able to advise you both.'

'Of course. I brought it with me hoping …'

She handed over a dark red and gold box. Mr Timpson examined the necklace closely until he found the tiny engraved sign he was looking for. He seemed pleased and nodded at Polly.

'Mrs Taggerty, this necklace is almost certainly worth rather more than you would expect to get for the pigs. If I were you I'd take it. It's valuable and very lovely.'

Mrs Taggerty was thinking. It's gold, real gold. Taggerty is such a miser. He never gives me anything. No jewellery, not even chocolates, nothing! So I'll have this necklace. And I don't care what Taggerty says! She took the necklace in its box.

'Thank you for your help, Mr Timpson. Goodbye Mrs Faraway. Goodbye Mr Faraway.'

'And now,' said Polly, 'Nick, quick. Paint off that "Less" from the sign. It's Hope Farm from now on. I'm off to tell the pigs.'

The pigs stood in battle order, heads raised, waiting. They had heard the sound of a car driving off. Shortly afterwards they heard the noise of a truck starting up and pulling away. And after that – silence.

They looked at each other, unsure. Was this a trick? Then, running towards them, leaping and smiling, came Polly. She dropped down on her knees before them.

'You're ours now, pigs, and you're here to stay. For ever and ever!

And the following month this advertisement appeared in the local papers:

Pigs Ploughmen

HALVE THE COST OF YOUR WEED KILLING · PLOUGHING · FERTILISING.

· ALL DONE ORGANICALLY BY A POWERFUL TEAM OF PIGS. KEEN WORKERS · FRIENDLY ·

COME AND SEE FOR YOURSELF AT

HOPE FARM, COXTON.

ASK FOR NICK OR POLLY.

THE REAL WORLD OF PIGS

PIGS ARE NOT WHAT THEY SEEM. Not by their own choice are they dirty and smelly. They earned this reputation from the way they were traditionally kept, often on a cobbled undrained floor in a small sty, just a lean-to against the farmhouse or buildings. There their dung heaped up in a corner of the open end of the sty, a corner carefully reserved for this by the pigs. They were, you see, doing their best to be clean. The rest of course was up to the farmer who could be pretty casual about the daily chore of cleaning the sty.

Pigs are really forest animals. To life outside that environment they are not so perfectly adapted. They have no coat of fur to protect them from the winter winds and cold or from the hot summer sun. Pigs are unable to sweat freely and easily become overheated, sometimes fatally. Once an archbishop's famous prize pig died on the eve of an agricultural show, not of stage fright, but of heat stress! In the cool, moist, calm of the forest shades, however, pigs are no longer handicapped. Miraculously, there in and under the forest floor lies all their food. Long ago when most of our land was covered by forest, pigs must have felt they owned the earth.

Today's pig has to make do with whatever shelter his keeper provides, good or bad. In a heatwave, if it only could, a pig would make for water or mud to wallow in, to roll in and cool off in 'mud, glorious mud'. It's true 'there's nothing quite like it for cooling the blood'.

Now a dirty pig is just one that has rolled most deliberately, most pleasurably, and of necessity, in mud. If only mud were Blush Pink or Spring Green, or any other nice decorator's shade, a pig might be labelled something funny instead. Those lucky pigs who spend their daytime out of doors, have (for me) an agreeable piggy smell, and still luckier pigs who have access to water delight in it. No wonder, for a pig is of the hippopotamus family and a hippopotamus spends his tropical days submerged in water up to his snout. Perhaps he cannot sweat either.

A friend of mine kept pigs for years. Her pigs were let out daily for two hours both morning and evenings. A river bounded her land. The pigs would splash around in it chucking stones about for fun. One day, she told me, they swam across the river and entered a church during a service. 'Ah,' said the priest with great presence of mind, 'the Gadarene Swine.' If you think that pigs swimming a river is a tall story, *The Beast Book for the Pocket* says a pig 'swims well without suicide'.

On an organic farm near Wexford, in Ireland, a

small herd of saddleback pigs has been used instead of a plough to clear areas of land that had lapsed into wildernesses of weeds and bramble. The pigs are enthusiastically digging it all up. There is a disc of gristle at the end of a pig's snout, backed by two extra bones in its nose, hardening it into an excellent tool for endless rootling, digging and probing in the earth for the pig goodies that lie within – the roots and the things that creep and crawl below. Meanwhile, the dung pigs drop is a rich fertiliser for the soil. Thus does a pig partly sustain itself with less cost and great benefit to man.

But its dung has earned it a bad name in Ireland because the slurry from a large intensive pig enterprise was allowed to drain into that great fishing lake, Loch Sheelin, and the fish died. Silage effluent or cow slurry might have done the same. Nitrates from the vast grain lands draining into Lake Eerie in Canada did the same. Fertilisers like these can set up a process in water called eutrophication. In simple terms, this means an explosive growth of green algae and phytoplankton drawing so heavily on the oxygen supply in the water that insufficient remains to keep fish alive.

Pigs are herd animals and have a basic need for the company of other animals, particularly pigs. That's why Runtling, in this book, who was removed from his pig family and kept in a small sty at Stubbs's farm, found life so unsatisfactory. Not all the straw or food a pig could want compensated for his boredom and loneliness. Of course, he was not thought of as a pet, but as an economic waste food converter. Farmers are inclined to take the view that if an animal grows and puts on weight, it is contented. Not so, there are fat unhappy pigs just as there are fat unhappy people.

Piglets that have been kept as real pets seem to have adopted the human family as 'other pigs' or 'other animals' in the way that dogs substitute their human family for the pack. A pet runt I know of was coming in and out of the house, going walkies, even travelling in a car, and if left behind showed positive distress.

Of all farm animals the pig is surely the most intelligent and communicative, but if it's an agricultural breed, its life as a pet will be sadly short.

These pigs can grow to a monstrous size. A large white boar can weigh up to 250 kilos (600 lbs) and a sow, 200 kilos (440 lbs), and reach over 2 metres (over 7 feet) in length. Imagine it in the house. More practical would be a miniature pig like the Korean Potbellied, sometimes found in Garden Parks for children. It remains the same size as a dog, I believe.

So how is life for the majority of pigs today, spent as it is from birth to death in the enclosed buildings of an intensive pig enterprise? Well, they are never hungry, although every meal tastes the same. Never too hot or too cold. And they are never without the close company of other pigs.

But within the sheds there is only one dominating smell and sound – that of pigs interrupted at intervals by one other, the sound of their attendants whose clothing already smells of pig. And there is only one unchanging view, that of other pigs in a grey uniformity of concrete pens and steel rails.

And what is lacking? There is no sight of the world outside this factory. Nothing really of the life a pig is equipped for. No room to move freely, except round other pigs in the same pen. No chance to satisfy its innate and compulsive need to dig and delve in the earth with its purpose-made snout. That must bother it a lot as it stands on its concrete floor. No opportunity to exercise its keen and discriminating sense of smell and hearing, which in a more natural environment would be sending quick-fire messages for its brain to interpret, and its body to act on, all the livelong day.

And to all of this how does it adapt, an animal with such lively sensibilities as a pig? How does it? I ask.

Linda Moller